By the Sea

Olivier Bonnewijn – Amandine Wanert

THE ADVENTURES OF JAMIE AND BELLA

By the Sea

MAGNIFICAT® • Ignatius

Table of Contents

Chapter 1
Where Do I Come from? 7

Chapter 2
Hidden in the Hull 15

Chapter 3
The Cry of the Gull 23

Chapter 4
Flashlights 33

Reading Key:
To Better Understand the Story 41

Chapter 1 Where Do I Come from?

Summer was nearly over, and Jamie and Bella's family were on vacation. The twin brother and sister had just pitched their tent near Highland Lighthouse. They were very excited to camp out by the sea! The sun was setting and slowly disappeared over the horizon. Dad went to fetch the kerosene lamp. He did not turn it on right away, letting the evening shadows slowly envelop the family. All was peaceful.

"When you kids were small, we often came here to this very spot," Dad said in a deep and reassuring voice. "Jamie and Bella, you would spend hours digging in the sand. Once you even set up a pastry shop on the beach to serve sand cakes with seaweed or shell toppings to every passerby."

"Yuck," exclaimed the twins' seven-year-old sister, Lily, making a face.

Dad looked at her gently and said, "You had just learned to walk. You waddled everywhere, squashing everything in your path, especially the twins' sand cakes."

"By accident, of course," Jamie added sarcastically.

Lily didn't even have time to snap back. Bubba, their four-year-old brother, jumped onto his father's knee and asked, "What about me? Where was I?"

"You weren't here yet," Dad answered.

"Where was I then?" Bubba repeated.

"Nowhere," Mom said, scooping up Bubba in her arms. "You didn't exist yet."

Bubba didn't utter another word. He snuggled close to his mother.

"Wasn't he in Heaven with God?" Jamie asked.

"No," Dad replied. "It may be difficult to picture, but instead of Bubba, there was nothing. Then one day he began to exist. God's love created him."

"God's love and ours," added Mom, looking tenderly at her husband.

Bella listened attentively. She did not want to miss a word of what her parents were saying. She didn't know why, but the words struck a chord in her heart.

It was bedtime. Dad had finally turned on the lamp. After kissing everyone goodnight and brushing her teeth, Bella slipped into her tent. Jamie and Lily followed.

Bella tried to fall asleep but couldn't. So many questions burned within her. She unzipped the tent and looked out at the stars twinkling in the sky. Their reflection lit up her dreamy eyes.

Jamie popped his head out of the tent as well. "What are you up to?" he asked.

"Nothing," Bella replied.

Lying next to each other, the twins silently gazed at the heavens, listening to the sound of the waves crashing upon the shore.

"So many stars," whispered Bella all of a sudden. "Where did they all come from? They didn't put themselves in the sky."

Jamie thought of what his mother had said—that he and his brother and sisters were made by God's love and his parents' love. He remembered his friend Popov, the homeless boy he'd met at the train station during another family vacation.

"Does he also come from the love of his parents?" Jamie asked himself. "He doesn't even know who his parents are. So, where does he come from?"

"Oh, look, a shooting star," exclaimed Bella excitedly. "Quick Jamie, make a wish!"

Jamie closed his eyes and thought of his friend. He longed to see Popov again.

Chapter 2 Hidden in the Hull

Just after sunrise, the twins made their way to the foot of the lighthouse. They wanted to fish. Lily came along too. As they walked along a dock, without warning Jamie stopped in his tracks. He stood motionless, as if struck by lightning.

He had just seen a boy who looked identical to Popov. He was standing on the deck of a large fishing boat.

"No, it can't be!" he thought. He wanted to cry out, but the boy had gone below deck.

"Why are you stopping?" asked Lily, staring at her brother.

"Are you already tired?" she teased.

"No," Jaime answered and pointed to the boat. "Up there I saw a boy who went down into the hull of that rusty old boat—it's Popov, I think. I'm almost positive. Let's go find out!"

The kids ran to where the boat was tied. They called out, but no one answered. Jamie, followed by his two sisters, bravely boarded the vessel. Once on deck, they climbed down into the hull, hoping to find Popov. The bottom of the ship was poorly lit by a single dangling light bulb. A fishy and oily smell filled the air. Lily grasped Bella's hand. She was trying to be very brave.

"Popov! Popov!" Jamie cried out, trying to speak over the loud whirring of the machines. Just then,

a hand grasped his shoulder, making him jump. Turning around, he came face to face with his friend.

Jamie's heart started to race.

"Popov! No way, I can't believe it! Last night, I was just—"

Lily's voice interrupted: "Hi! I'm Lily, and here's Bella!"

"Helloo," answered Popov, smiling. He was touched. He motioned them to follow.

"With me you come."

Breathless, the kids followed their guide into the bowels of the ship. The group weaved their way through all kinds of nets and wiring, steel beams and ropes. They arrived at an area filled with old anchors. This was Popov's hiding place.

"Nobody knows I here. No documents. Afraid police find me," he said, quivering.

Jamie became more and more curious. "But how

come you are on this boat?" he asked.

Remaining silent, Popov handed over an old photograph.

The picture showed a young girl of about fifteen leaning against the wall of a small hotel. Seated on a low window sill beside her was a little boy with auburn hair. A little further, in the entryway of the inn, stood a man in a white lab coat and a woman, both with blurry faces. Jamie read the words on the back of the photo: "Cry of the Gull. Cheddar Island."

"Parents I know not," explained Popov. "I looked Internet 'Cheddar Island'. I found. I come. Me learn English."

All of a sudden, the children heard voices on deck. Sailors had come aboard. They didn't dare show themselves and remained in hiding. They didn't want to betray Popov. Suddenly, the ship's horn blew loudly. The vessel left the dock and headed for Cheddar Island.

"Dad and Mom will worry," sighed Jamie anxiously. "And there's no way to let them know we're here. You okay, Lily?" he asked.

"I'm a little scared, but I'll be all right," Lily said as she tried to fake a smile.

Seated on an old sack, Jamie felt uneasy. What kind of adventure were they embarking upon?

Chapter 3 The Cry of the Gull

The boat docked on Cheddar Island an hour later. The children disembarked without being noticed by the crew. They found the Cry of the Gull hotel shown in Popov's photo. It was falling apart. The walls were moldy, and many of the shingles were missing from the roof. Old shutters partially hid the dirty and half-broken windows. Mustering up the courage, the kids pushed

the door open. It squeaked loudly. As they entered, they bumped into a grumbling old woman in the hallway. Her features hardened as she looked at them. She seemed cranky.

"The coffee shop is closed to street urchins," she said, raising her raspy voice.

"Hello, ma'am," Jamie answered calmly. "Do you recognize the people in this picture? It's really important."

Showing her displeasure, the old woman put on her glasses and examined the photograph. Her beady eyes lit up.

"Ma'am, sorry to bother you, but could I have a glass of water or some juice?" Lily asked as politely as she could. "I'm thirstier than a dinosaur," she added.

"Annah. Annah," the lady murmured aloud without paying any attention to Lily. "It is Annah," she mumbled to herself.

"And there, the little guy, he's her step-brother,

Popov. They lived here for about a year," she said.

Popov was deeply moved by her words. His face was shining with hope. He asked, "And others? Who are they?"

"I don't know," answered the lady, adjusting her glasses and looking closer. "Ah yes, these people

came and took Annah and Popov away. They left without saying where they were going."

Just then, a man with a big moustache burst in and shouted, "Shut up now, woman! Stop gossiping, and you kids, get out of here before—"

"But sir," Jamie said, courageously stepping toward the man, "we just needed some information. Look here at the photograph—"

Before he could continue, the man ripped the image out of his hands. He tore it to shreds and threw the pieces on the floor. With clenched fists, he advanced toward the kids yelling, "Get out! Get out, you brats!"

The children ran out and hid behind a hollow tree opposite the inn.

"What a meanie," Lily whispered as tears rolled down her cheeks.

"We must get back to Mom and Dad right away," said Bella. Popov stood still. He just stared at the

old house. Countless emotions stirred within him.

Suddenly he jumped at the slam of a door. The man was leaving the inn and walking hurriedly down the street. Without a moment's hesitation, Popov stealthily crossed the street and slipped into the building.

Wanting to help, Lily followed impetuously. Jamie and Bella chased after her, and the three entered the inn together. They found Popov seated at the kitchen table with the old woman.

"Here you are," she said, smiling at Popov. "I taped your picture back together. I knew you would come back." She paused briefly to look at Jamie, Bella and Lily. "Don't bother about the owner," she continued. "He's not a bad man, but he can be grumpy."

Popov looked at the lady kindly and gently took his picture back. He then pointed to himself: "Me, Popov."

"That I had guessed," said the woman. "You were

three when I saw you last. Annah waited on the tables here, and she took care of you."

Popov bit his lips, trying hard to understand every word. Luckily, Bella had a great memory and concentrated hard so that she could remember what the woman was saying.

Jamie stood by the window on the lookout for the owner, who could return at any minute.

"Address Annah, you have?" inquired Popov eagerly.

"No, I'm very sorry," the old woman answered.

Popov closed his eyes. All of a sudden, he felt very lost and alone in the world, abandoned by everyone. A black cloud whirled within him. He felt short of breath.

Sensing his sadness, Lily wanted to cry but held back her tears. She inched closer to Popov and nudged her shoulder against his to comfort him.

Then she asked, "Ma'am, can you give Popov

a glass of orange juice? He looks so sad. Pretty please?" She smiled coyly at the woman and added, "Um, and I'm thirsty too."

"Uh-oh," shouted Jamie. "The owner is on his way back here."

"Quick," cried the old woman, "go out here through the kitchen door."

"Bye-bye! Thank you!" the children called over their shoulders as they hurried out.

The children ran as fast as they could back to the dock. Thank goodness they found a ferry back to the mainland before their parents could worry about them.

Chapter 4 Flashlights

An oil lamp's warm glow lit up a corner of the Highland Lighthouse campsite. Jamie and his father finished washing the dishes in the basin. Bubba was whining because he couldn't find his teddy bear. Mom turned on her headlamp and went to prepare a sleeping arrangement for Popov. She had been touched by Popov's story and kept on thinking about his torn picture.

"How could she comfort him," she wondered.

She grabbed her wallet, took out an old picture and went straight to Popov. It was a photograph of her and her husband, his arms wrapped around her. She looked at Popov and spoke soothingly, using hand gestures so as to make herself better understood:

"Though I didn't know it yet, I was pregnant with Jamie and Bella when this photo was taken. They were there and no one knew, not even me. Only God knew. And He already loved them infinitely. It is He Who had created them."

Somehow, Popov grasped the meaning of these words. He took the picture in his hands and observed it at length. As he was looking at it, he was flooded with peace.

Bella, while tidying up her tent, had overheard everything. She too felt peace enter her heart. She sometimes wondered if her parents had really wanted her. They wanted a baby, of course, but they

hadn't expected twins. Those first few months after she and Jamie had been born couldn't have been easy! Now she understood—she was a gift of God's infinite love, like Popov. It was God Who had loved her and created her in secret.

Just then, Lily popped her head into the tent.

"Hey, it's me!" she said. Lifting a bottle of orange juice, she added, "I brought this in case I got thirsty. Can you make some room for me, Bella?"

Before waiting for an answer, Lily squirmed in next to Bella, who hugged her little sister. "I'll be right back," Bella said as she stepped out of the tent to wish her parents good night.

On her way back, she realized she had not seen Popov.

"Jamie, have you seen Popov?" Bella asked her brother, who was hanging up wet towels.

"No, I haven't. Let's go look for him."

Using their flashlights, the twins searched their

surroundings. Soon they found Popov seated on a
boulder, looking out to sea. He was thinking of his
parents and of Annah, his stepsister. He knew that
here on earth he would probably never meet them
again. Tonight, however, this painful thought did
not disturb him. Tonight, he knew where he came
from. He came from the love of God.

His heart was now filled with hope. Moving his

lips slowly, he silently prayed the Our Father in his own language.

"Oh, Popov! You're here," said Jamie, placing his hand on his friend's shoulder.

Bella sat next to him and added kindly, "You know what, we'll try to help you find your family. Perhaps one day—"

Popov interrupted her: "Me thank you."

The children fell silent and listened to the soothing sound of waves crashing against the rocks. The clouds cleared, revealing the starry sky above. Tomorrow would be sunny.

To Better Understand the Story

1. **Where was Bubba when Jamie and Bella were small?**

He did not exist as such. However, God had always known He would create Bubba. Even before He created Bubba, God knew him and loved him. He waited for the moment when he would give Bubba life.

2. Why does Jamie find Popov again?

Is it because his wish was granted when he saw the shooting star? Probably not. Is it mere coincidence or pure luck? Perhaps. Could it be a gift of Providence? What do you think? Is there a difference between coincidence and Providence?

3. What is Popov searching for?

Popov is searching for answers to many questions that have troubled him for a long time: "Where do I come from? Who are my parents? Do I have brothers and sisters, uncles and aunts? Am I loved?"

4. Who are the people in Popov's photograph?

Is Popov's father the man in the white lab coat? Why is he dressed like that? And the woman next to him—is she his mother? What were they doing on Cheddar Island? What became of Annah? Neither the reader nor Popov can answer these questions. He must have been very disappointed. There are very few clues in this story, but perhaps he will find his family one day.

5. How does Popov find peace at the end of the story?

Thanks to Mom's words of wisdom, Popov now knows that he was created by God's infinite love. This certainty is as solid as the rock on which he sits when he prays the Our Father.

6. What does Bella discover at the end of the story?

Like Jamie, Bella likes to ask questions: "Eleven years ago, Mom and Dad wanted a baby. But did they want me?" That night, Bella understood that God wanted her and created her out of infinite love.

7. How can I pray to my Creator?

Below is a beautiful prayer from the Bible. You can also pray it or write one that resembles it:

For you formed my inward parts,

you knitted me together in my mother's womb.

I praise you, for I am wondrously made.

Wonderful are your works!

You know me right well;

my frame was not hidden from you,

when I was being made in secret,

intricately wrought in the depths of the earth.

Psalm 139: 13–15

The Author   Olivier Bonnewijn

Father Olivier Bonnewijn has been a priest of the Archdiocese of Brussels in Belgium since 1993 and is a member of the Emmanuel Community. He teaches at the Institute for Theological Studies in Brussels.

The Adventures of Jamie and Bella were conceived during summer catechetical camps. The children's thirst for truth and their contagious enthusiasm inspired the stories, which are all based on true accounts. Father Bonnewijn had the joy of witnessing many of them.

The Illustrator   Amandine Wanert

Amandine Wanert lives in Paris. She illustrates both for medical journals and for children's literature. Fascinated by the world of children, she spends time observing them in public parks and in school settings to fuel her imagination. Jamie's and Bella's physical features are in part based on her childhood memories. Bringing to life The Adventures of Jamie and Bella in harmony with Father Bonnewijn's text has been a joyful and enriching experience for Amandine.

Translated by Marthe-Marie Lebbe
Cover illustration by Amandine Wanert

Under the direction of Romain Lizé, Vice President, MAGNIFICAT
Editor, MAGNIFICAT: Isabelle Galmiche
Editor, Ignatius: Vivian Dudro
Assistant of the Editor: Pascale Vandewalle
Layout Designers: Élise Borel, Jean-Marc Richard
Proofreader: Cameron Pollette
Production: Thierry Dubus, Sabine Marioni

Original French edition:
Les aventures de Jojo et Gaufrette : Au bord de l'océan
© 2010 by Édition de l'Emmanuel, Paris

Printed by Tien Wah Press, Singapore
Printed on January 2014
Job Number MGN 14000
Printed in Singapore, in compliance with the Consumer Protection Safety Act of 2008.